For PT

All rights reserved. For information about permission to reproduce selections from this book, write to trade.permissions@hmhco.com or to Permissions, Houghton Mifflin Harcourt Publishing Company, 3 Park Avenue, 19th Floor, New York, New York 10016.
www.hmhco.com

The illustrations in this book were done digitally.
The text type was set in Chaloops and Eatwell Chubby.
The display type was set in Eatwell Chubby.

ISBN 978-0-544-96635-2
Manufactured in China
SCP 10 9 8 7 6 5 4 3 2 1
4500679487

My Toothbrush Is MISSING!

JAN THOMAS

Houghton Mifflin Harcourt

Boston   New York

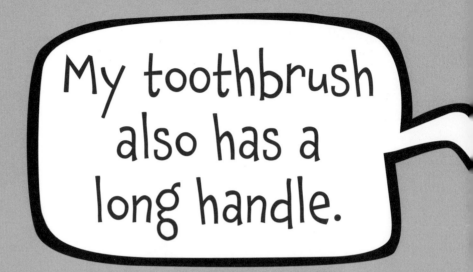

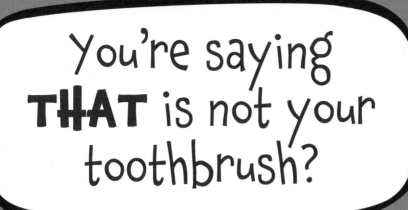

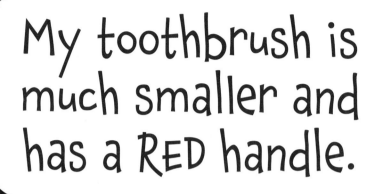

My toothbrush is much smaller and has a RED handle.

Red. **Weird.**

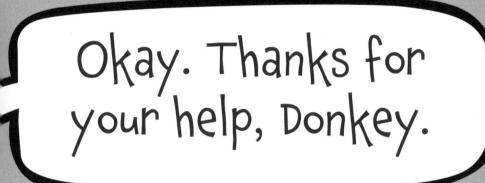

Okay. Thanks for
your help, Donkey.

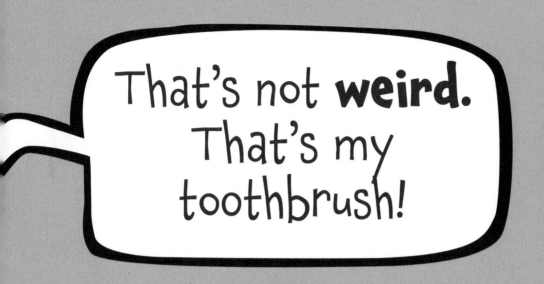

Looking for more laughs?

There's a PEST in the Garden!
JAN THOMAS

My Friends Make Me HAPPY!
JAN THOMAS

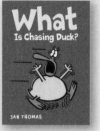

What Is Chasing Duck?
JAN THOMAS

Get your child ready to read in three simple steps!

1 I READ	Read the book to your child.
2 WE READ	Read the book together.
3 YOU READ	Encourage your child to read the book over and over again.